# A Parting Shot

**Also in this series of new poetry and fiction from LinguaBooks**

No Means No
The Legend of Sidora
The Taste of Rain

# A Parting Shot

and other twisted tales

Maurice Claypole

**LinguaBooks**
www.linguabooks.com

Paperback edition: ISBN 978-1-911369-55-4
eBook edition: ISBN 978-1-911369-56-1

First edition

Editor: Ann Claypole

Copyright © 2022 LinguaBooks

A CIP catalogue record for this book is available from the British Library.

Maurice Claypole has asserted his right under the Copyright, Designs and Patents Act, 1988 to be identified as the author of this work.

This is a work of fiction. Any resemblance to actual persons, living or dead, or actual events is purely coincidental.

LinguaBooks
Elsie Whiteley Innovation Centre
Hopwood Lane
Halifax HX1 5ER
www.linguabooks.com

Beneath every story, there is another story. There is a hand within the hand… There is a blow behind the blow.

— Naomi Alderman, *The Power*

# About this book

This collection of twenty-one delightfully odd and quirky tales will transport you to times and places ranging from the familiar to the unexpected, from the extraordinary to the surreal, from the world we ourselves inhabit to imaginary realms where anything can happen.

Within these pages you will find tales of betrayal and retribution, love and devotion, tragedy and murder. Be prepared to expect the unexpected as life-affirming stories are intermingled with tales from beyond the grave.

Step into a world where nothing is as it seems.

# Table of Contents

# Preface

Many of the strange and unexpected events related in these pages arose during the telling as the characters I created seemed to take on their own lives, often heading in directions other than those I had originally mapped out for them.

It is this sense of the unexpected that I wish to impart to you, the reader, in the hope that you may share my wonderment at the little twists of fate that govern all our lives, at the shifting borderline between the world we think we inhabit and the world as it may actually be – a dimension in which things are rarely what they seem, a world in which reality has gone slightly wrong.

I invite you to join me in a journey of discovery and share my surprise at each tangled twist and turn in these tales of ordinary people whose only crime is their human nature.

Maurice Claypole

# A Parting Shot

'Try this. It's really special. Like an ultra-powerful Becherovka with a hint of Angostura.'

'No, I can't. Really. I'm driving.'

'One for the road, then,' Benny indicated the line of shot glasses and exotic liquors lined up on the kitchen counter of his rather over-stylish ground floor apartment.

'OK. Hit me,' Frankie acquiesced. 'It's been a rough ride, but at last it's all settled. The deal of a lifetime. They've received the merchandise and have transferred the balance to our account. And by the time the banks close tomorrow, the transaction will be final, so nothing can go wrong now. And if anything happens to either of us before we receive confirmation tomorrow, the other can take control.'

'Yeah, it's been great working together, but now that we've scored the big one, it's probably best if we don't meet again.'

'A parting glass, then,' said Benny, closing his laptop.

'A parting glass,' echoed Frankie, sliding his sleek black tablet into its protective cover.

Of course, Frankie was not his real name, any more than his partner in crime was actually called Benny. In the circles they moved in, no-one used their real names if they could avoid it. In his younger days, Frankie had borne more than a passing resemblance to one Francis Albert Sinatra, and Benny had briefly owned a couple of restaurants, so the duo's double moniker was quickly established as a given.

As he turned and headed to the door, Frankie smiled to himself; he was secretly proud of his finesse. He had guessed that the last glass would contain a modified form of the puffer fish venom, tetrodotoxin, known to insiders as TTX. After all, that is what Benny had used on the old man all those years ago. For Frankie, it was a simple matter to switch the glasses.

Although he had done well since his days as a strong-arm man, as far as Frankie was concerned, Benny was so predictable, an amateur. He was trying to be sophisticated by parading his collection of shot glasses from all over the world and proffering them to sample the various brands of exotic hard liquor he had amassed on his travels and kept on display in a glass wall cabinet. But what Benny, despite all his feigned airs and graces, didn't know was that he was already a dead man.

'Bottoms up!'

'Down the hatch!'

They say that as you approach death, you acquire a sixth sense, and maybe it was that, or maybe he had caught Frankie's expression reflected in the glass door of the display cabinet, but in an instant, Benny was cursing himself. He didn't know how it had happened. Oh, he knew Frankie was good and had half expected him to try the switch, but was sure he wouldn't get away with it. After all, each glass was different and he was sure he hadn't taken his eyes off the drinks for a second, but somehow, the other guy had done the switch anyway. Benny couldn't taste the TTX, but a strange feeling in his gut told him something was wrong, and he was already having difficulty focusing.

He knew that it would take several hours for the venom to take full effect, causing paralysis and ultimately death. There was no cure. And even if he was wrong, even if Frankie had downed the deadly shot, there was no harm in making sure. He felt the weight of the cool steel in his pocket as he followed Frankie to the door.

Frankie was still musing to himself over his sleight of hand – tip the contents of Glass A into empty glass C, then Glass B into glass A and finally Glass C into Glass B. So even if the glasses were marked, Benny was going to get his comeuppance. Of course, this called for an extra distraction, neatly provided by entering the wrong code into his laptop to cause Benny's tablet to ping a menacing warning before Frankie put things right, in more senses than one. Tricky, but hey, when it came to sleight of hand, Frankie was the master, after all.

Frankie passed through the doorway, pulled his collar up against the cold, and then half-turned with a wry smile on his face, 'See you later, alligator.'

'Yeah,' replied Benny, raising his pistol, 'in hell!'

— ༒ ༒ —

# Vigilance

The call came in at just after 3 am. Detective Zeke Raziel, known to his friends as Raz, because for some reason, nobody liked to call him Zeke, typed in the details that would send a squad car round to what appeared to be a 10-16 domestic disturbance. The department was short-staffed, so Raz was filling in on despatch duty. When times were busy, they wouldn't even respond to a domestic unless there was a clear indication of threat to life and limb, but it was a quiet night and unit Delta 22 was quickly on its way. Sergeant Shaun Adams and Constable Walter Trimble were expecting to find a feuding couple who in the meantime had calmed down, stopped the shouting that had aroused their neighbours and probably hit the sack and gone to sleep. But that's not what they found. To Raz's mind, they found something much worse.

No, there were no signs of violence, no blood-spattered walls, no occult messages, nothing of that sort. In fact, nothing at all. Absolutely nothing. An empty apartment, not a single item of furniture or clothing. Nothing. Nada. Blotto. Zilch. But what the hell, no crime either, so Adams and Trimble logged it as a domestic that could not be pursued any further: 10-16 disregard incident. Dossier closed.

Except that for Raz this was not a closed dossier. It was very much an open one. Back at his regular desk, he tapped his pencil against a blank notepad and contemplated the framed sign he had hung on the wall, a reminder to 'Be sober, be vigilant', a motto he strove to live by. Sobriety was a big ask in the police department, and as a serving officer, he often got ribbed for his abstention, but more than that, it was the vigilance part that dominated his nature and which motivated him to look closer into just such cases as this one.

The pattern had been repeated three times in recent weeks. A reported disturbance at night, quarrelling couples or family members, then nothing. All gone. Nothing there. No explanation.

With no crime and no threat of one, it was not police business, but that would not stop Raz from following up on this case in his spare time. He was a lifelong fan of mysteries, strange tales and the unexplained – everything from UFOs to spontaneous combustion. He had painstakingly researched them all, reluctantly but successfully debunked most of them, and still kept a dossier on the few for which explanations were still outstanding. Like the disappearances in Precinct 13.

The pattern was always the same: some kind of disturbance, usually late at night, followed by an unexplained and seemingly impossible disappearing act. Individuals vanished into thin air, their prize possessions gone. Occasionally some old remnants of earlier years remained, an odd item of furniture, an ornament, a photograph or two, but nothing of value. Without a victim and a list of missing items, an incident of this kind could not even be treated as a burglary; no case, nothing to investigate.

Nothing to investigate – officially. But Raz had his own agenda and was free to pursue each case in his own time. As a rule, the neighbours who called in the disturbance were reluctant to talk and, in many cases, did not even identify themselves when they called, but this time it was different. The incident had occurred in a well-to-do gated community dotted with neat detached houses, each snuggling safely in its own extensive grounds surrounded by trim lawns and herbaceous borders.

You would hardly expect the sounds of marital strife to reach the house next door, let alone give cause for alarm, and yet their immediate neighbour, a Mr Olam, was parking his car at the time and clearly heard voices raised to the deafening volume of impending violence and promptly called the police. And the next day, he was perfectly willing to receive a visit from Detective Raziel and fill in the details.

Ushering Raz into an expansive and tastefully decorated lounge, Olam seated himself in a high-backed club chair near the marble hearth and motioned Raz to take the matching seat opposite. He was of indeterminate age, well past middle age and yet not elderly, a head of white hair, full and flowing and yet neatly trimmed with a well-groomed beard to match. He smiled jovially as he poured them each a drink from a crystal decanter. Raz could not recall the beverage being offered, or himself accepting, but it was just a soda and tasted just right.

'So,' ventured Raz, 'what can you tell me about the incident last night?'

'Ah, yes, the incident,' mused Olam, almost to himself, 'I'll tell you what I can, and I will do my very best to be accurate, because I fear that very often the devil is in the detail.'

As the old man told his tale, it transpired that the couple next door, Henry and Frieda Randall, were not shouting at one another but at a visitor with whom they seem to have entered into some kind of agreement. It appeared that he had come to collect his fee for past favours rendered, but the Randalls were insisting on being given more time.

Enquiring about the Randalls' past life, Raz found that they matched the pattern he had observed several times before. All the individuals and families concerned had done surprisingly well for themselves: a slow start in their chosen careers, then sudden success, riches piling up and then poof, all gone.

As he took his leave, Raz had the feeling that he had in fact given him more to go on than a mere witness statement and that this might not be the last time they would meet.

Handing over his card, Raz ventured, 'I know it's a long shot, but if you see him again, will you give me a call?'

'I will,' said Olam, 'and please forgive my curiosity, but I would likewise be grateful, should you ever find him, if you would let me know.'

Following this interview, there was only one thing Raz could do, but it was something he was quite good at. He waited. In any case, the next few days were filled with paperwork, routine inquiries, an occasional genuine 10-16 or 10-31 crime in progress, but nothing that related to this case or its parallel manifestations. In fact, he was immersed in the routine police work of filling in forms and cataloguing data, when he noticed someone standing in his peripheral vision. He glanced at the glass door of his office. He did not recall it being opened or anyone passing through, and yet there was now a tall, dark figure standing in front of him.

'Allow me to introduce myself,' said the stranger, holding out a warrant card, 'Agent Beliel.'

Raz couldn't quite make out the details on the card, but it seemed to indicate that his visitor was some kind of federal agent. Raz straightened up in his chair and assumed the 'officiously polite' manner he reserved for dealing with potentially troublesome members of the public and self-important politicians.

'How can I help you?'

'More to the point, how can I help you, Detective Raziel? I am here to make you an offer.'

There was no hint of a threat in these words, on the contrary, they were uttered in a soothing, mellifluent tone that put Raz at ease and dispelled the initial frosty tension of the exchange. Raz remained silent. Sometimes patience brought its own rewards.

After a moment, Agent Beliel continued, 'A proposition, you might say. My sources tell me you have been a mere detective for over seven years now, despite an impeccable record and no small measure of success. And it's so difficult nowadays to make ends meet on a detective's salary. Would you be interested in, let's say, "upping your game"?'

The proposal was indeed intriguing. Raz listened intently as Agent Beliel set out the details of the proposed agreement, venturing at length to ask, 'So how do we – er – conclude this agreement? Do we sign something?'

'Oh, no,' said his visitor, in a tone that sounded like he wanted to add the words, "dear boy", but held himself back at the last minute, 'we simply shake hands. What you may call a gentlemen's agreement. It's the physical contact, you see, that is worth so much more than merely signing in … er … ink.'

'I have an alternative proposition,' said Raz, fixing his gaze directly into the deep dark eyes of his interlocutor. 'There is someone else you should meet. Someone more important than me.'

'Your superior? I'm afraid you're a little late for that. Lieutenant Lucas and I already have a long-standing arrangement.'

'No,' replied Raz, 'this person is much higher up. I can set up a meeting if you like. After all, what have you to lose? We can always carry on our discussion another time.'

To Raz's pleasant surprise, Agent Beliel actually seemed quite taken with the idea.

'Yes, why not?' he murmured in dulcet tones that seemed to betray the thought, 'two birds with one stone, not bad for a day's work.'

A brief phone call set up the meeting and Raz logged himself as off-duty before leading his visitor to the precinct house car park and hitting the road for a certain gated community.

As they entered the house, Olam showed them through to the spacious lounge, but this time, he remained standing, thanking Raz for the introduction and addressing his tall dark visitor directly.

'I understand you have a proposition for me?' he enquired, listening politely as Beliel once again set out the details of his proposed agreement.

When Beliel had finished his pitch, Olam held out his hand.

'I think we have a deal,' he said.

With a satisfied smile playing on his dark features, Beliel took the proffered hand, which gripped his so firmly that Beliel uttered a piercing shriek of agony, his twisted mouth contorted by the throes of realisation and anguish. He tore his hand away, but too late. His cry reached a deafening crescendo as a blinding burst of flame engulfed his entire being, hovering there just long enough to hear his adversary utter a final admonishment.

'I think you misunderstood me there,' said Olam with a severe but benevolent smile, 'I meant that we already have a deal. An agreement we reached long, long ago and a debt which I am now calling in.'

And with that there was a final clash of sound and light as the air closed in on the space that had been occupied by Agent Beliel.

Turning to Raziel, his faithful angel, Olam became his former jovial self.

'Thank you for drawing my attention to this. He's been on the loose for a long time, but generally not too much trouble. However, it seems he's been a naughty boy recently, so I've sent him back to where he came from.'

The next day, Raz made discrete enquiries and found that the Randalls had returned, together with all their possessions – as had each of the other victims of sudden disappearance. In fact, hardly anyone had even noticed they were gone, except for him. Their friendly old neighbour, however, was nowhere to be seen. Raz had promised to refer Beliel to a higher authority, and you can't get any higher than that, but clearly Olam didn't need to hang around any longer. For ordinary mortals, as it were, the incident had been wiped out. Case closed. Job done.

Things were quiet that day in Precinct 13 and as the sun went down, Raz volunteered for an extra shift on despatch and settled down in his chair, looking forward to a quiet night.

The call came in a little after 3 am.

*Be sober, be vigilant, for your adversary the Devil like a roaring lion walketh about seeking whom he may devour.*
(I Peter 5:8)

*What harmony is there between Christ and Belial? Or what does a believer have in common with an unbeliever?*
(II Corinthians 6:15)

# Damaged Goods

'There you go, love. Just sign here."

The portly delivery driver handed over the package and held out his mobile device for her to sign. Andie wiggled a long, pointed a nail at the touch screen and tried to manage a smile.

'What's the name, love?' queried the courier, peering at the screen.

'Andrea Symonds, same as on the address label.'

'Righty ho. Have a nice day, love.'

Love, love, love. There was no love involved, but it was the local way of addressing people, relatives, friends, customers, passing acquaintances and even total strangers. No love involved, she mused wryly to herself, or perhaps there was. Perhaps that's as good as it gets. She watched Mr Love, surprisingly fleet of foot for his weight, skip back down the front steps to the garden gate, making sure he closed it properly before taking the parcel through to the kitchen.

It wasn't the only reason she had taken the day off work, but it made a change to receive a parcel in person rather than find a card in her letterbox and pick it up from the counter at the corner shop, which is the way it was often done nowadays. There was something reassuringly normal about having a parcel handed over on the doorstep; it was the way things used to be, the way they ought to be.

Placing the box on the kitchen counter, she noticed a slight dent in one corner. It didn't look too bad but judging by the general state of the outer packaging, it had received quite a bashing here and there. Still, she hoped the contents would be OK – a hanging planter for the front porch; she needed some colour there – lobelias, perhaps, or a trailing mix of petunias, calibrachoa and ipomoea – something to brighten her day on entering and leaving the house.

She stared at the package for a moment, then steeled herself to attack the grey plastic outer packaging that had recently replaced brown paper as an outside wrapper for cardboard boxes. Reaching up, she carefully took down the kitchen scissors from their prescribed hook on the rail above the sink, just next to the sharp knives neatly arranged in order of size. Her mind was awash with the feast of colour the flowers would bring to the tiny porch as she snipped her way through the untearable plastic and stripped it from the cardboard box inside, which, although duly dented, seemed strong enough to protect its valuable cargo.

She replaced the scissors on their hook and inserted a fingernail under the paper tape used to seal the box, a technique she had used dozens of times before, but either the tape was stronger on this occasion or she used too much force, or for whatever reason, her nail broke, a sliver hanging off like a scraggy shard of her shattered personality.

'Drat!'

Somehow, she sensed that this might be some kind of ill omen and reached for a sharp knife to cut through the tape, momentarily dropping the knife on the floor.

'Drat!' she uttered again, 'Drat, drat drat!' Her strict Methodist upbringing forbade the use of stronger oaths and curses, but there were times when she nearly slipped.

Now she saw from the smiling corporate logo on the side of the box that she had it upside down. It shouldn't really matter, but it bothered her all the same. She liked things to be just right – not upside down or in the wrong place, but just as they ought to be. It was when she turned the box over that she noticed a faint rattle coming from inside. Placing it securely on the counter, she sliced through the tape, opened the box and peered inside. It seemed full of shredded cardboard, the modern substitute for bubble wrap and polystyrene peanuts. Was it really better, she wondered, to cut down trees to make paper packaging than to use some form of plastic? Ah, yes, recycling, she told herself. That's what it was all about, but somehow, she didn't quite believe it. And it didn't work. As she lifted out the ceramic hanging planter, she could see that the rim was chipped.

She stared at the place where a centimetre of porcelain had flaked off the surface, interrupting the decorative pattern. She could probably hang it so that the damage was out of sight, but that was not the point. In a way, the chip added a variation to the pattern, making it unique, but again, that was not the point. It just wasn't *right*. And where was the other one? She had ordered two identical planters, one for each side of the porch. What good was one without the other? She needed symmetry, not chaos.

The planter wasn't the only thing that was damaged. She cast her mind back to last night's confrontation. She had tried to let the business with the parcel drive it out of her mind, but it was still there, nagging at her, tugging at her psyche. What had started out as a perfect evening had quickly turned into a disaster. Well, maybe not quickly but, it seemed to her now, inevitably. Her friends had often taunted her for being old-fashioned, but was it her fault if she had standards? Bill had been sweet. Bill was perfect – well, as perfect as she could imagine any man could be – loving, attentive, kind, sensitive to her needs and they had grown steadily close together. She had suspected that the romantic candlelight dinner at the Riverside Restaurant would mark a special occasion of some kind, and in her heart of hearts, she had suspected what Bill had in mind. He was well aware of her love of the traditional, her conviction that things had to be done right, that everything had to be just the way it ought to be; a time and place for everything, everything in the right place and at the right time.

But by the same token, she could not allow herself to hope, anticipate or prejudge anything that had not actually happened yet. Bill had chosen the perfect location, the perfect moment, but even he could not avert the inevitable disaster.

When, after a pre-prandial rumba to the gentle strains of the resident band and a delightful four-course meal, exquisitely cooked and tastefully served, Bill produced a glittering diamond ring nestling enticingly on the plush cushions of its dedicated presentation box and sank onto one knee beside the table, taking her hand in his, her heart leapt with the joy of the moment. But then she was seized by an involuntary sharp intake of breath as the horror welled up inside her and took over.

'I can't,' she said.

Bill was thunderstruck. This was clearly the one thing he was not prepared for.

'But…,' he stuttered, 'I don't understand…I thought this is what we both want. I'm asking you to…'

She tried to speak, but the words would not come. She wanted to say, 'I know what you're asking, and I want to say yes, but…' She wanted to say a hundred things, and yet she couldn't. Bill, seemingly now also speechless, resumed his seat at the table, slipped the ring box into his pocket and poured her a glass of water.

Then the dam burst. In a fit of tears, she explained why she could never marry him, never marry anybody. She knew she was being stupid, she knew she was old-fashioned, she knew that the world wasn't like that anymore, but she also knew how she felt inside: unclean, spoiled, sullied.

She told him the whole story. Of the abuse, the rape, the horror of unspeakable acts of brutality, of the agony she carried with her at all times, suppressing it only in the rare moments of happiness she had known during their time together.

'But that's all in the past,' he tried to soothe her, to show that he understood, that he didn't care about that, that he loved her now, as she is today, that he loved the woman she will always be. But to no avail; she was sobbing bitterly; people were looking; everything was ruined. It was so simple, really, she couldn't let a lovely man like Bill ruin his life by marrying a wreck like her. And that's when it happened.

He was clearly hurt, but still the perfect gentleman, sweet and loving, understanding, reaching out a familiar hand to wipe a tear from her cheek, when she exploded.

'Leave me alone,' she spat at him and again, at the top of her voice, 'Just leave me alone' and her hand shot out and slapped his face with the full force of her pent-up frustration, a sharp nail scouring a deep gash across his cheek.

Stunned, Bill just sat there, cheek reddening, a trickle of blood slowly snaking down his face. He stared at her open-mouthed for a moment, then looked around the restaurant to see that they were the centre of attention and felt the looming presence of a bow-tied waiter sternly approaching their table. Bill pushed his chair back, threw his napkin on the table and stormed out of the room. As she watched him go, Andie was paralysed by the sensation that he was storming out of her life forever.

Smoothing the crumpled delivery note onto the countertop, she took out her mobile to tap in the number of the sender. A hotline, a call centre, an automated voice, a series of decisions to make, numbers to punch in, then a ringing tone, a long wait and finally a human voice, annoyingly smooth and mellow.

'Hello, my name's Janice. How can I help you today?'

'I want to complain about a delivery.'

'What seems to be the problem?'

'There's no *seems to be* about it. I ordered a ceramic hanging planter and it's chipped.'

'Was the damage caused in transit?'

'How do I know? Either it was like that when you sent it, or…'

'Was the packaging intact?'

'Yes, no… it was dented.'

'You should always check the parcel for damage before you sign for it, madam, otherwise we can't claim against the insurance.'

'That isn't my problem. I want what I ordered and what I did NOT order was damaged goods.'

Andie realised she was on the verge of shouting and tried to collect herself, 'And there were supposed to be two planters. I only received one.'

'According to our records, two were dispatched at the same time. They would be packed separately. Did you receive a second parcel?'

'No, I didn't! Otherwise, I wouldn't be complaining, would I? And I had to wait ages before getting through...'

She was working up to a full volume rant now, but Janice interrupted smoothly, 'No problem, madam. I'll contact the driver and ask him to check for the second parcel and get it to you right away.'

'Yes, but...'

'And about the chipped ceramic, madam. If it's only a minor defect, I could arrange a discount if you would prefer to accept it as it is.'

'No, I can't accept it as it is. It's ruined!'

She knew it wasn't Janice's fault, but it was like yesterday all over again. The flood gates opened and a torrent of oaths prepared to come out of her mouth, but her anger turned to sobs and tears welled up in her eyes as Andie's voice choked up and the words died in her throat.

'No problem madam,' replied Janice smoothly. 'We'll send you a replacement right away. And I can confirm that the second parcel will be with you shortly. Is there anything else I can do for you today?'

'Is there anything else I can do for you today?' Andie mimicked sarcastically, 'You can give me a new life, that's what!'

In years gone by she would have slammed down the receiver, but the best she could do on her mobile was stab a broken fingernail at the screen to end the call.

So there was a second parcel. She would have to go through it all again.

She caught her breath when she heard the doorbell. This time she would open the parcel before signing for it. If Mr Love had to wait, that was his look-out. In fact, she thought she might give him a piece of her mind anyway. It was his company that had somehow managed to destroy her precious planter in spite of its packing. She flung open the door, sharp words of confrontation on the tip of her tongue. It was Bill.

Andie stopped in her tracks. She knew it was Bill, but she could hardly see his face, for in front of it he held the most exquisite bunch of orchids she had ever seen, lusciously adorned with monstera leaves and anthurium. If there was one thing she loved more than orderliness and tidiness, it was flowers. If there was one thing she loved more than flowers, it was Bill. He held out the bouquet which she instinctively, almost as in a dream, accepted, lowering the blooms to let their fragrance waft up to her captivate her senses. This in turn revealed their bearer, a sheepish smile on his face.

'I brought you some flowers,' he said unnecessarily, 'I just wanted to say – if you will still have me – I don't care about the past. And I hope it's the same for you. If you'll let me in, I have a confession, too.'

Suddenly, all the pent-up tension came out and she fell into his arms, squashing the orchids between them, but she just didn't care.

'Yes, yes,' she said, 'I don't give a damn about the past – whatever you have done, it can't be worse than what would happen to me if we were never together again.'

Still standing in the open doorway, he held her close, stroked her hair as her head rested on his shoulder. Behind him she perceived a rapid movement. It was the delivery driver, Mr Love, placing a parcel just inside the gate, sensitively reluctant to come any closer.

'I'll just put it here, love,' he said, 'I missed this one earlier. No need to sign for it again.'

'Wait!' she called, the prepared complaint welling up inside her for a brief moment, then she relaxed. 'Never mind,' she said, 'It's fine.'

And as she watched the delivery man carefully close the gate and step out of her field of vision, she said to herself, 'Perhaps, sometimes, damaged goods aren't all that bad.'

# The Patch

There were two bodies in the alleyway. Clearly, it had been a shootout, but no-one could work out quite why. The deceased were both members of the same gang and were not known to be rivals. The word was that they were like brothers and were both doing very well out of the local business. Things had never been so good on the Patch, everything was under control, stuff was bought and stuff was sold; everyone knew their place – and yet, there had clearly been harsh words, threats and ultimately, violence and fatalities. A third person was present, sixteen-year-old Daj, but clearly, he had not fired a shot, nor had he taken any part in the aggro that preceded the bust-up.

'If you want to know who did it, look at who's left,' said DI Kestrel, turning away from the crime scene and ducking under the police tape. He had seen enough and was heading back to his car as fast as his legs and his weight would allow.

'Yeah,' said DS Dunnock, himself no spring chicken and struggling to catch up, 'but he's just a kid. He wasn't involved. We have witnesses who heard every word of the slanging match between the other two. He's in the clear.'

Nevertheless, Daj was duly interviewed, at home and in the presence of his single and protesting mother, and subjected to subtle threats and coercion within the limits permitted by law, but his story checked out. His version of the escalating argument matched that of witnesses who had overheard the fracas. For the time being at least, the detectives had drawn a blank.

Retiring to his room, Daj turned to his favourite book. It was in times like these that he sought solace and remedies in the book. The book had helped him through many a hard time. The book was his refuge, his mentor, his response to the sorrow and anger of life on the Patch. He immersed himself in the book and began to feel the hurt and the injustice fading away.

Further witnesses were sought, forensic evidence obtained, but there was nothing to shed new light on the case. Nothing that is, until the pattern repeated itself a couple of weeks later. This time, the remaining members of the local gang were wiped out by out-of-area rivals intent on taking over their turf. And again, Daj was present, even though for most of the time he seemed to be hiding round the corner of the dark alley where the incident took place. Unable to explain his presence to the satisfaction of DI Kestrel, he was taken into custody, but once again, there was neither evidence nor testimony to indicate his involvement, so he was duly released with a stern warning not to hang around the gangs.

'Gangs, what gangs?' he answered, 'They're just guys from the hood. They used to be my friends. I don't know about no gangs.'

DI Kestrel was intrigued by the phrase 'used to be' that Daj had let slip. He was sure there was something there and determined to dig deeper. When records showed that the kid's elder sister had died from a drug overdose the previous year, Kestrel had him picked up once again. But to no avail. So the boy had a motive. So what? Many families on that block had a motive. That proved nothing. Again, Daj was free to go. Back home, Daj turned once again to his favourite book to find a modicum of solace.

The third incident eliminated the newcomers who had moved in on the Patch and took the death toll to new heights. It was seen as a warning to rival gangs to leave the Patch alone, and indeed, after this no-one else tried to move in or carry on the 'business' anywhere within shooting distance. For the first time in a generation, the Patch had been swept clean. The newspapers had a field day with headlines about gang warfare, and some even speculated about a mysterious vigilante literally 'going gangbusters', but in the weeks and months that followed, the whole episode faded from the public memory and whilst a police spokeswoman assured the media that the 'investigation was on-going', the dossier was, for all intents and purposes, closed.

In his room, sitting beside the framed photograph of his then smiling sister, Daj once again, maybe for the last time, took out his favourite book, lightly running his finger over the embossed lettering on the cover which read, 'Ventriloquism Made Easy.'

# Goodbye to Old Fort Niagara

If it were only one box it would not be so bad. But there were dozens of them: big, cardboard boxes so heavy it took two people to lift them, smaller ones whose size was not problematic, but the contents of which certainly were; and then there were the shoe boxes. Why people always collected letters in shoe boxes he was not quite sure, but he guessed that it was not just the size; there was a kind of intimacy in a shoe box, as though each one somehow held a tiny part of the soul of everything that had ever been hidden away in a shoe box: secret little trinkets too precious and personal to throw away, lead crystal carefully packed in cotton wool, a furtively stored firearm, and above all, letters: letters no-one would ever read again, but which were too intimate, too full of confidential outpourings, too packed with declarations of love, hate and frustration, too heart-rendingly filled with expressions of joy, happiness and misery, to cast into the flames.

He pushed aside the shoe boxes and drew one of the big brown packing cases towards him. Delving in, he pulled out a piece of paper at random: a map of Old Fort Niagara. Immediately, the memories flooded through him: Sandra standing by the walls of the fortress telling him about the Canadian invasion, the two of them walking through the nearby park and finally himself, alone, gazing over the lake in the early morning mist before crossing the border into another world. A deep, involuntary sigh accompanied his movement as he placed the map on the floor, starting one of the two piles he planned to make, one for 'keeps', the other for 'throw aways'. Whether it was the pile of 'keeps' or the pile of 'throw aways' he was still not sure.

Next out of the box was a theatre playbill from London, bearing the title 'Firedance' in crimson: a show at the Haymarket that had run for only a few weeks before being hastily replaced by a re-run of 'Hair'. Time had completely erased that day from his memory, but now it all came back, every song, every dance step of that show so long ago. The playbill was now a valuable piece of theatre history. He placed it on top of the map of Old Fort Niagara and thrust his hand back into the box.

But after an hour or so, he found that instead of the two piles he had planned, he had just one stack of papers, containing all the contents of the first box. The heap continued to grow as he worked his way through the second box. Hours later he had a single mound of paper and a collection of empty cartons. Through a kind of mental torpor, he gazed at the shoe boxes for what seemed like ages before pulling the first one toward him and lifting the lid.

The first letter was from Jennifer and contained a photograph of her in her new home, smiling at him across the miles, across the years. His eyes closed as something moist ran down his cheek. Carefully inserting the letter and the photograph back into its envelope, he placed it on top of the mountain of memories.

Finally, the shoe boxes, too, were empty, discarded around and the single heap of paper. He felt tired, worn out as though emptying the boxes were like emptying his soul onto the floor. Standing up, he made his way slowly to the door, casting a last look at the heap in the middle of the floor and inviting empty boxes all around. That was all that he could do today, he thought, as he gently closed the door behind him: tomorrow was another day.

As he descended the stairs, there came from the other side of the door a faint rustling of paper, the almost imperceptible sound of stacking and ordering, of lids gently closing, of cartons reclaiming their precious contents.

# Riding the Storm

Shadow's haunches stiffened as the charging horde approached; Lord Ryder held him in check with the reins. 'Steady, boy, steady. Have faith'. Glistening with sweat in the midday heat, the stallion threw back his head, harrumphed his weather-beaten lips and stamped a solitary foot in trepidation, but steadfastly held his ground. The deafening roar of the onslaught was nearly upon them when a blanket of fire flew over their heads from behind, a storm of blazing arrows piercing, scorching and scattering the onrushing vanguard and driving the back the thundering phalanx. The stifled battle cries gave way to screaming, commotion and the horror of retreat. In no less time than it had taken the barbarians to launch the attack, they had turned and fled, leaving behind a heaving tapestry of trampled bodies and burning flesh.

A deft flick of silver spurs and a gentle tug on the bit caused the old warhorse to turn away from the carnage and trot slowly back to the fortress. It was over. At least for today.

For ten years now, Lord Ryder had held the barbarians in check, preventing their repeated attempts to assert their false claim to his ancestral lands. Indeed, it was ten years to the day since his father, on his deathbed, had passed on to him the one true sword, known in his tongue as Durandur, the Avenger or throughout the Old World as Palamandes, the Righteous. By any name, this was not only the symbol of his power, but a fearsome weapon, a curved tracer that could slice through flesh on contact, requiring little or no pressure in the fulfilment of a just cause. He had long since ceased to carry the blade in battle, preferring to display its symbolism on a silken sash above his throne as an assertion of his heritage and a visible reminder of his rightful position as leader of his people.

With a final glance at the charred battlefield, he turned his faithful steed around and headed back to the encampment, pausing briefly to recoup at an outlying tent before returning to the royal yurt.

As she helped him out of his armour, Lady Doranda, Royal Consort and since their marriage, co-ruler of the United Lands, breathed the traditional welcome, 'Again, Milord returns. May it ever be so' although the last sentence seemed faint, her husky voice almost lost in the breezy expanse of their canvas palace.

'Strong drink and a goodly wife to return to,' he replied, 'And speaking of strong drink...'

'As Milord wishes,' she smiled dutifully, 'but first, sit and rest' and as he did so, she busied herself behind the throne, pouring the celebratory wine.

'Did I see you enter Magda's tent on the way back from the affray,' she asked, and since there was no reply, continued, 'it seems you also sought her blessing yestereve before the battle. Is that so?'

'That, dear wife, is no business of yours. Let it rest. You have vowed to obey me and obey me you will. That is all you need to know.'

Standing behind him, gently caressing the nape of his neck, then his cheek, Doranda persisted in a tone both soothing and firm, 'Indeed, I may let it rest, Milord, but first assure me that there is no truth in the rumour that of late you have frequently sought more than a blessing from our noble High Priestess.'

'Let it rest, woman! Bring me drink and grant me rest, too; at the end of battle, I need respite from cares. Obey and do not question!'

This outburst was met by a brief pause and a rustle of silk as Lady Doranda uttered the gently reassuring words, 'As you wish, Milord. My duty is to obey, and I shall grant you the rest you deserve.' And her hand swiftly drew the sharp blade of Durandur the Avenger across his throat.

# No Man's Land

Standing on the unseen border of the potential site, Harper consulted the description on his mobile device, pausing a moment to take a snapshot of the seemingly barren area before him. Clearly a prime location; sites like this were few and far between these days. In many cases, there were unsurmountable planning issues, transport difficulties or infrastructure problems, but there seemed to be no obvious reason why this particular spot had never been built on.

His gaze took in an extended patch of grass; short, tufted turf of what must be a very hardy variety. His research had revealed the land to be unsuitable for cultivation but just perfect for new housing stock, maybe even a retail development. He always liked to assess a new site from the edges before pacing around and across it to get a full impression of its extent and periphery, but on this occasion, he found it difficult to focus, perhaps, he told himself, because there was nothing to focus on.

But the more he looked, the more it seemed that an area at the centre had been flattened.

He returned briefly to his car, took a sip of rapidly cooling Costa coffee and secreted his tablet and briefcase under the front seat, keeping only his jotter with its little resident pencil in order to take old-fashioned notes if he really needed to, which usually he didn't. On jobs like this he liked to keep a clear head and remain unencumbered; he wasn't one to take dozens of unwarranted photos just for the sake of it. It was a notion that went back to his early training: don't take notes, take note; and he had also learnt that taking photos stopped you actually looking at what you had in front of you. Observation, not photography, was his job. It was his recollections that would go into his report, his impressions, filtered through his many years of experience and expertise. And yet, there was something elusive about the empty space before him.

He briefly shook his head to clear it and proceeded to walk around the perimeter. Two and a half acres of prime urban land, he mused to himself. At today's prices that would return a commission of... but a movement in the corner of his eye interrupted his thoughts. Turning his head, he espied a figure standing next to the agency 'For Sale' sign. Again, he found it difficult to focus, but after a moment, he could just about make out a tall man with distinct features wearing what could be a military dress uniform – or maybe that of a brass band – not unlike Sergeant Peppers but well worn and faded – and holding a glittering top hat in his hand. Ah, yes, thought Harper, there was always a brass band playing somewhere in this northern town. That would be it. Or a drum major of some kind. Now the stranger was standing in front of him. He was taller than he had seemed at first, with a distinctive beard. He somehow reminded Harper of Uncle Sam on stilts.

'Are you interested in this land,' asked the stranger, speaking in what could best be described as a quietly booming tone – no more than a whisper and yet betraying a deep and sonorous timbre, a sotto voce bass voice.

'Er, yes. My agency specialises in urban greenfield sites.'

'Would you like to see more?' Asked the tall gentleman, deftly placing the top hat on his head.

As he did so, the light seemed to shift, the colours of his tunic becoming brighter and his deep blue eyes taking on a radiant sparkle.

'Er, well, yes, but I don't suppose there's much to see.'

But Uncle Sam, the drum major, or whoever he might be, was already striding away, tracing the circumference of the site. Harper felt obliged to follow. 'There really isn't anything here. I just wanted to get an impression of the area,' said Harper, quickening his pace to catch up.

'There's this,' said the man, indicating the round canvas tent that Harper had not noticed before. Wasn't that the spot with the flattened grass, he thought. It must be a trick of the light that he had failed to see it before. They were progressing around the perimeter at quite a speed but also circling inwards towards the centre of the site, so maybe he was disoriented; yes, that would be it.

'I forgot to introduce myself,' said the "drum major" as he lifted the flap on the tent, 'My name is Barum. Please step inside.'

Inside the darkness of the tent, the sense of expectation was high. There was a buzz amongst the families seated around the large sawdust circle; children with ice creams, apple-red faces and big toothy smiles and babes in arms fidgeting in their mother's lap, when suddenly, the whole area lit up and from somewhere a band struck up a marching tune. Barum stepped into the centre of the ring and boomed, his voice a whisper no more:

'Welcome to Barum's Big Top. The Greatest Show on Earth. Put your hands together for our star riders!' And as he began to clap rhythmically, the whole audience picked up the tempo, building to a crescendo until suddenly, through a flap at the opposite side of the ring, a rider on horseback – dressed in a white sequined riding suit and hat, burst onto the scene. Then another horse and rider followed, then another, forming a dizzying circle of equestrian magic.

And there was more magic: the magic of the flying trapeze, of airborne conjurors, whirling gymnasts, animals large and small, camels, elephants and tigers, death-defying lion tamers, hilarious clowns, strong men, sword swallowers and fire eaters, an amazing spectacle that had the children cheering, the adults gasping with wonder and Harper struck motionless by the sounds, the sights, the sparks, the smell of sweat and animals, of smoke filling the air, clogging his nostrils, choking his throat until amidst the ensuing panic, he lost consciousness.

Coming to his senses, Harper could still smell the smoke, the sawdust, the animal dung, the perspiration of the performers, but as his vision cleared, he once again found himself on a piece of barren land. Yes, there was a patch of grass in the middle that was depressed – and possibly charred – a circular spot where nothing grew now nor ever would again. He took out his faithful jotter and next to the name of the plot, wrote the words, 'Not suitable for development. Do not purchase.' As he headed back to his car, he had the feeling that he was being watched, and turning back to look, he fancied he saw a tall distant figure raise its top hat in a gesture of thanks.

# Goose in Straw

As they lingered over a leisurely Sunday breakfast, Darren looked up from checking his phone.

'Any messages?' asked Sarah.

'Auntie Nora's sending us a goose,' said Darren.

'You're joking!'

'No, that's what her text says: "Goose in straw on its way to you now. Karen is bringing it over."'

There's one in every family and as far as far as Sarah was concerned, the mad one in their family was Darren's Auntie Nora, who kept chickens and a bewildering variety of other poultry in the back yard of her old farmhouse and grew just about everything imaginable on her allotment. It was not unusual for her to send them garden produce unannounced and extremely welcome when she sent them a turkey at Christmas, but you never knew what was coming next and on one occasion she had inexplicably sent them a litter of kittens. It was preceded by one of her brief text messages to say that she was sure they would love the little dears or find them a good home. Auntie Nora never wasted anything, and she certainly never wasted words.

'What on earth will we do with a goose?' asked Sarah, 'There's no room in the freezer.'

'Er… she says, "goose in straw", so I wonder if…'

'Oh no, you mean she's sending us a live goose? That's impossible. She knows we've only got a tiny back yard. And what on earth will we feed it on?'

'Well, we'd better get ready. She says Karen's on her way right now.'

So Darren and Sarah abandoned their leisurely breakfast and spent the next two hours creating space in the backyard, fixing the fence and even cleaned out and repaired the old rabbit hutch that had spent the last twenty years rotting in a corner of the back yard.

They were feeling really pleased with themselves when Karen's Land Rover pulled up outside and Karen came up to the front door carrying a basket.

'Is that it?' asked Darren anxiously, as Karen lifted the cloth covering her basket to reveal… six jars of strawberry preserves with added gooseberry, but labelled simply, 'Goose in straw'.

# George

George watched as the sea receded, slowly ambled back into the cover of the bushes and slept. It was hard to say in those days, whether George dreamed or not, since the only thing to dream of was the cycle of life on his island, the warmth of the sun and the coolness of the sea. Day after day, George watched, slept, ate and watched. He was in no hurry.

He watched as the first boat landed and tall strangers got out and began to erect strange structures that flapped in the breeze and into which the men disappeared at night. There was much activity during the day and from time to time the men would take fish from the sea or go inland and return ladened with carcasses. And they liked fire. George knew about fire; he had seen the forest burn more than once. Fire was dangerous, it could hurt you, but these men seemed to like the scorching heat; they made their own fire, fanning the flames until they grew high, gathering round the burning pyre to eat. George watched them eat.

Day after day, he watched them come and go, watched as they grew older and died and watched as the structures fell down and the sea came inland and washed every trace of them away.

The next fleet of ships brought a bustle of men and women who cleared part of George's homeland, erected solid structures in its place – houses, workshops, trading posts – and then there were oxen and horses and more activity, things moving at a pace to which George was unaccustomed. The oxen spent little time grazing and most of the time pulling and hauling. The men sat on the horses and sometimes the horses drew large carriages, transporting goods, supplies, people further inland and returning with more of the same. There were things even taller than trees, things that blocked out the sun and cast long shadows, causing George to find a new spot from which to observe all these changes.

After some time, he noticed carriages that moved all on their own, without the need for horses or oxen, but made more noise and emitted strange noxious smells. A honking and shouting filled the air and there was more noise than George had ever heard before. And things moving faster than anything he had ever witnessed. And smells that made no sense, had no meaning, but burned his nostrils. And most strange of all, he had to move further away to find the night, for the night did not come where all this fuss was going on. The sun went down, but there was no real darkness and often, the stars could not be seen. In those days, George began to dream of quieter times when the only sound was the sound of the wind rushing through the vegetation, the hiss of the surf on the sand and the only sources of light were the warming sun and the crisp clear moonlight.

The new inhabitants did not seem to like the sun or the moon, but more than anything, it seemed, they liked fire. There was more fire than he had ever seen, and if he ever got too close, there was more heat than he had ever felt from the sun. Sometimes the fire stayed and burned, and sometimes it came in quick bursts. And the noises became louder and more frequent, too, deafening booms that shook the air, and a rapid rattle that ripped the peace apart, often followed by loud wailing noises and a sense of things and people darting about in every direction at once.

But the assault of sound and movement was not just taking place on the land. George craned his neck to look up, guided by the ominous drone of objects in the sky, followed by an even more deafening burst of sound and the heat of fire, the smell of burning. The buildings crumbled, the noise died down, and after a while all was peace again. For some time after, George would dream of the strange noises, smells and sights he had witnessed, but then the dreams receded as it all passed into history and he all but forgot about those strange hectic days.

George watched as the sea receded. He ate, slept and watched, enjoying the peace that had once again descended on his island, an island he had lived on for over three hundred years. After that brief period of change, everything had long since returned to normal, and it was on a day like any other when George gazed out one last time at the serene sea, listened to the surf gently lapping on the sand, drew his long neck into his shell and closed his eyes for the last time.

— ೩ ೪ —

# Fairytale of West Sussex

Keith was on a creative hiatus but would have still been on a high if he wasn't well into the downers at the time. John spent most of the evening spaced out in a lotus position, eyes wide behind those round specs, gently mumbling to himself. Yoko hadn't turned up, so it fell to Anita to sit with him from time to time, uttering soothing words and occasionally replacing the beer in his hand. Charlie had left early, off to team up with some old pals at Ronnie Scott's. It could have been any one of a number of similar occasions at Keith's Redlands estate in West Sussex except that there was a constant hubbub of expectation, everyone (well, maybe not everyone) was secretly on the alert. I guess it was well after midnight when Mick clapped his hands. 'OK, you guys – about the tour, I've got an announcement to make...'

As for me, I already knew I was on the forthcoming stateside tour. As a sound engineer, you get to work quite close to the band at times; at least you get respected – you are involved in the music, unlike the endless stream of agents, lawyers and PR people, who seem to make up most of the Stones' entourage. You are doing creative work – and you get invited to the parties – well, nobody actually gets invited, if you're a familiar face, you can just turn up. You just have to fit in. That's my special talent. Whereas extroverts like Mick dominate a room as soon as they enter, I'm mostly invisible. Even if I were a big star, most people probably wouldn't recognise me.

But the announcement wasn't about the tour as such; for the band, it was much bigger than that. This would be history in the making. But you have to be really into the blues to understand. The Stones had always been a blues band. As I write, some 40 years later, they still are. Chicago had always been on the cards, but the suits wanted everybody straight in and out, no hanging around. But now Mick had overcome legal and financial objections to wangle an extra day in Chicago and, yes, Muddy Waters would be playing at the Checkerboard Lounge. A cheer went up at this news. Dropping in at the Checkerboard mid-tour was the blues equivalent of a pilgrimage to Mecca. The guys had first met Muddy in the summer of

1964 when he was painting the ceiling at Chess Records on South Michigan Avenue. Muddy had heard the Stones on record and thought they were black.

I was standing next to Anita when Mick broke the news, and although she already knew all about it, she joined in the delight and gave me a big hug. For a brief moment I held the most fascinating woman in the world in my arms, drawn into her aura, her perfume enveloping me. It seems impossible now to express the power that emanated from her in those days. Imagine the Kardashians all rolled into one, then double it and morph them all into a stunning, mystical blonde. Brian, Keith, Mick and many others had all fallen under her spell at one time or another.

It was a fleeting moment. I've worked with lots of bands over the years, been to more parties than I could possibly remember, done a lot more than hug on many occasions, I can tell you – hell, I've got six grandchildren – and yet it was that one brief moment with Anita Pallenberg when time stood still.

— ❧ ❧ —

# The Blue Lamp

Constable Dixon was glad to be back on the beat. He caught a brief glimpse of his face reflected in a shop window as he took in the familiar sights and sounds of the high street. Now in his mid-fifties, he was even beginning to resemble his television namesake of yesteryear. His colleagues at the station had long-since stopped making fun of his name, although new officers would almost automatically ask, 'When are you going to make sergeant, George?' But he was used to that and would just respond with a kindly smile, touching his forelock in a mock salute, and utter Jack Warner's famous catchphrase, 'Evening all,' and the joke would be over.

Life in the station was one thing, but the real job was here, out on the streets. Modern community policing (and probably budget cuts and a shortage of cars) had put bobbies back on the beat, although today's officers looked nothing like the traditional notion of a 'bobby', since nowadays, they were all kitted out in fluorescent vests and bristling with equipment, a far cry from the days of Dixon of Dock Green, and yet Constable Dixon yearned for the simplicity, the camaraderie, and even the sense of justice that had prevailed in those days. Maybe one day, whilst making an arrest, he might even hear the immortal words, 'It's a fair cop, guvnor' that embodied the spirit of the TV show. He smiled at the thought.

In a way, it was a miracle that PC George Dixon had ever made it to the small screen, having first been killed off in the movie, The Blue Lamp, but you just couldn't keep a good copper down. That was true then, and it was true today. Dirk Bogarde had gripped audiences and made headlines with his portrayal of the dashing young anti-hero in the movie, but it was law and order that the elderly George Dixon had stood for, and it was law and order that Constable Dixon was doing his best to enforce right now.

He weighed up the two suspects approaching him; they were certainly familiar, but he could not quite place them. There was something furtive about their manner.

'Hello, George,' said the taller of the two, dressed simply in what seemed to be a light topcoat over a suit, or at least a collar and tie of the everyday workwear variety.

'Evening,' replied George cautiously, planting his large feet firmly on the ground, ready for anything that might ensue, 'can I be of any assistance?'

There was a pause as the three of them each seemed to assess the situation. Then it was the smaller man who spoke, softly but with a threatening urgency: 'We'd like you to come with us,' he said. He was dressed more casually than his companion, his clothes loose despite a stocky frame and muscular neck. He looked as though he was no stranger to trouble. George hesitated before opening his mouth to find some soothing words, when a third voice from behind caused him to turn round; a woman's voice:

'I'll take it from here.' With relief, George realised it was another police officer, one of the modern breed, blonde hair tied back in a short pony tail, walkie-talkie affixed to her high-vis tunic, a utility belt strapped around her ample waist.

'Let's all go down to the station,' she continued, but George protested.

This was all going wrong. He wanted to finish his round, make sure that everything and everybody was safe on his beat, find a kind word for any innocent vagrants, move on any unsavoury characters hanging about street corners and check the shop doors to make sure they were locked, like the second-hand shop they were standing next to just now. Once again, he caught sight of himself in the shop window, but this time he saw himself full length. His uniform was gone. No helmet, no tunic, no high-vis vest. Only the woman was wearing any kind of uniform. She placed a kindly hand on his arm. The two men kept their distance, but they seemed anxious, poised, just in case.

'I don't want to go to the station,' mumbled George, uncharacteristically unsure of himself, but gazing in the direction from which he had come.

'No problem, George,' said the taller man. 'We'll take you home. Your tea will be ready by now.'

George Dixon, aka George Cawley, turned squarely to face his capturers, holding out his wrists as if to receive handcuffs. 'OK,' he said, 'it's a fair cop. I'll come quietly.'

And with that, the incident was over, and Constable George Dixon returned quietly to continue the investigation in the Blue Lamp Nursing Home, where his tea was indeed ready and waiting.

# Layers

Saskia elbowed the back door closed, her hands out of commission, struggling with the stacked pile of trays and boxes she had just brought in from the vegetable patch at the back of the house. Unloading her precious cargo onto the kitchen counter, she wiped her brow with a soiled hand, sweat dripping from her brow as a result of a day spent toiling outside on that rare occasion in the North of England, a scorching hot summer's day. She separated the trays and boxes according to their contents and surveyed her harvest.

Strawberries, of course, at this time of year, were part of her haul, not only a symbol of tennis at Wimbledon, but something quintessentially English in so many ways. Without even being aware of her actions, she selected a big, juicy specimen, rinsed it briefly under the tap and, holding it by the stem, bit into the blood-red fruit, deliciously firm and yet so sweet, with just a faint acidy aftertaste. She licked her lips, savouring the flavour before swallowing, then popped the remainder of the berry into her mouth, biting it off just below the stem, which she discarded into the composting bin under the sink.

Having rinsed her hands under the tap, relishing in the cool, refreshing water on her skin, she turned her attention to the rest of the gathered produce: two boxes of fine green lettuce, one tray of shallots, one of Japanese onions and half a tray of garlic. She set the greens to one side, their next destination being the safe, cool environment of the pantry, and began to prepare the onions and garlic for hanging from the storage hooks on the kitchen wall, just below ceiling height, binding the shoots and creating hanging loops, a delightfully repetitive process that occupied her time and focused her attention whilst at the same time enabling her to muse about her wonderful kitchen garden, her delightful family and life in general.

She was blessed with a truly wonderful exist-ence and was blissfully happy with her home life, a loving husband, two beautiful children as the fruit of their marriage and even a delightful little Pomeranian who answered to the name of Ollie, a happy, snappy four-legged friend now dozing lazily in his basket, tired out after an extended run-around with the children in the front garden.

Some time later, the garlic and the bulk of the onions hanging on their designated hooks, she set about preparing the vegetables that would form part of their family dinner later. Taking a sharp knife, she made two swift incisions into one of the largest onions, slicing off the shoot at the top and the root eye at the bottom, before starting to peel off the outer layer of skin, firm and silky, gossamer thin and yet so strong, so tough, a powerful sheath for protecting its precious core, but not itself destined for the cooking pot.

As she discarded the outer layer onto the worktop, her mind drifted back to the start of her day, Jamie supine next to her, snoring ever so gently. He would be wanting his breakfast. As she rubbed her eyes, finding it difficult to focus at first, a faint thrumming at the back of her head reminded her that it had been a late night. Yawning, she slipped silently out of bed, taking care not to wake the sleeping giant, and headed to the bathroom.

The second layer of skin seemed just as tough as the first, so she added that one to the small pile of discards forming on the counter and began to remove a third layer. She hadn't been late with breakfast, whatever Jamie said. He liked his fried breakfast prepared just right, eggs sunny side up and runny, toast still hot and accompanied by fresh coffee, and she was an expert at all things culinary, and an expert in pleasing her strong powerful husband, providing him the vital fuel he needed for his hard day ahead. But juggling with a menu of cooked and fresh ingredients took time and sometimes, it was hard to meet the morning deadline. Jamie liked his breakfast to be ready at eight o'clock on the dot. He would take his seat at the precise moment the minute hand pointed straight up, and this morning, she had been behind time, toast and coffee not ready, butter and preserves still standing on a tray in the kitchen.

She removed another layer, then another, the pile of outer skin growing, but the onion itself did not seem to be getting any smaller. 'Well, of course,' she said to herself, 'they are extremely thin layers.' It wasn't so much that he thumped the table in anger, sending silverware and porcelain jumping up into the air, but the look of loathing he gave her as he grabbed his jacket and headed for the door, snarling, 'You know I have to catch the train at half-past. And now you want me to set off on an empty stomach!' The door slammed and he was gone.

She stared at the growing layer of onion skin; there seemed to be more skin on the counter than there was onion in her hand, and yet the core of the bulb she was holding had become no smaller. A noise behind her made her turn. Patty was standing in the doorway, her tiny, uneven frame leaning against the jamb, 'Mummy,' she said, 'why are you crying?'

'Not crying dear. It's just the onions. They do that to you.'

'Do veggiesh make you cwy?' Patty pronounced the words slowly; her slurred speech had recently become worse, but Saskia was sure her lisp was improving. Patty's jaw hung open, wide eyes waiting for a response.

'Sometimes,' replied Saskia, peeling away another layer.

'Are ver veggiesh that make you larf, too?' asked Patty.

Saskia thought about this; there were veggies that made you smile, certainly, veggies that tasted good, but ones that made her laugh, she wasn't sure about that. Ah, yes, maybe, ones with odd shapes, naughty shapes. She laughed silently to herself as she removed another sliver of skin and added it to the pile. She used to laugh a lot. When Peter was still here, when they would run through the fields with Ollie, chasing balls and sticks, careening and gambolling gleefully across the grass as Patty sat on a park bench and watched, her pearly laughter adding to the joy as she wiggled her calipered legs about and pretended to run too.

This was becoming too much. Saskia was now certain that there was more skin on the table than there had ever been on the bulb itself. And yet the layers kept on coming. It was after they had said goodbye to Peter, as soon as they arrived back home from the church, that Jamie's mood swings had started. Well, you could understand that. Wearing black for a six-year-old would send any father to distraction. Saskia was so busy trying to console him that her own heartache somehow became absorbed into his pain, at least until later. She scooped up the shredded layers of onion skin and put them into one of the trays. It was almost full. She closed her eyes for a moment, steadying herself against the worktop, feeling the burdensome weight of the object in her hand. When she opened her eyes, Patty was gone.

Turning her head, Saskia caught sight of her own reflection in the darkened glass of the microwave, the swelling on her cheek a prominent reminder of the row the night before, a drunken brawl in which Jamie had blamed her for ruining his life, for neglecting their children, for being too busy to notice that Peter had gone down to the pond, and she had lashed out at his infidelities, a neighbour up the duff with his child and his selfish obsession with work and routine. As she pirouetted away from the vision in the dark glass, her foot caught a discarded wine bottle and sent it skidding across the tiles to rest with its fellows, all drained of their contents before Jamie got home late last night, himself reeking of booze and stinking of stale tobacco.

She stared at the hard round vegetable she still gripped firmly in her palm and reached for a sharp knife, determined to slice it to bits, to cut sideways through the layers, to end its dominance of her thoughts and actions, but however hard she tried, the knife just slid off the hard skin and she started to chop, chop, chop at it, but to no avail. The third time the knife slid off and sliced into her fingers, she gave up and stood there, now observing for the first time, that a trickle of juice was forming from the bulb in her hand, a tiny drip of acid landing in one of the cuts on her finger. She winced in pain as she began to peel away another layer.

They had tried to rescue Patty first, of course, but the smoke had already filled the house. Snuggled up tight with Ollie in her arms, she was already an empty shell by the time they carried her limp body down the ladder. Jamie, asleep in a drunken stupor, had fared no better, quickly reduced to cinders in the inferno.

As Saskia stared at the onion in her hand, all the outer layers were now stripped away, the core shrinking in her hand, getting hotter as the smell of roasting garlic, shallots and scallions and other bulbs of the Allium genus filled her nostrils.

Flames leapt from the hob, acrid fumes rapidly billowing as the curtains caught fire, invading the throat and lungs of the ephemeral being that had once been a woman called Saskia and who now, as on every visitation to this patch of charred earth, felt the once bulbous vegetable in her translucent hand fade and crumble into nothingness.

# The Way of All Flesh

Known to his friends simply as Hans and priding himself on being a fun-loving and approachable guy, he had to admit that he had made a comfortable living out of meat.

And despite having no lack of business acumen, he still liked to get back to the roots and kept a stall in the Borough Market where he still worked at weekends – not every day, of course; he had assistants who ran the stall most of the time. But at four o'clock on a Saturday afternoon, he could be seen deftly slicing chops from a carcass, dicing stewing steak or throwing oddments into the mincer. And always with a cheery smile, shouting out the last-minute special offers to his favourite customers, the shoppers of downtown Halifax. Like him, they understood the basic economics of supply and demand and knew a bargain when they saw one.

At home, too, Hans loved to spend time in the kitchen, bringing his big meat cleaver down on the chopping board; thick, juicy steaks, pork cutlets and lamb chops were his favourite, and he would throw them into the frying pan and watch them sizzle as his wife Dora busied herself with the vegetables and laid the table.

'How did you get on with that new contract?' she said, one evening as they were preparing their dinner in the usual way.

'Don't you worry about that,' he said. 'It's all sorted.'

'But you said that your competitor – what's his name – Spiro – was going to take the Aldi contract away from you and stop you getting that new Tesco order, too. We need the income, what with the expansion you've planned for the New Street Cold Store.'

'I know,' he said, 'It was a problem for a while. But you know me. I always get my way in the end. You see, Mr Spiro has gone away.'

A faint smile passed across his face as he slapped a piece of brisket onto the block. It quivered for a moment under the sheer force of his big hands.

'So don't worry,' he added, allowing his cleaver to hesitate ever so briefly high above the trembling flesh, 'he won't be back.'

Then with a resounding thud, he brought the heavy cleaver down on the block.

# The Photograph

Moira tucked in the sheets and patted Doris's hand.

'Is there anything else you need before I go?' she asked.

'No thank you love, I'm fine,' said Doris, 'I'm getting the jab next week, but my grandson Mike's picking me up, so it's all sorted. It'll be nice to get out for a change.'

Moira removed her apron and began to slip on her coat. She had been caring for Doris for three months now and had come to admire her good humour and tenacity. Doris had been blind for over thirty years and was almost bedridden, except for a few hours each day spent in her wheelchair.

'It's our anniversary today,' added Doris. 'That picture of Frank on the wall was taken forty years ago today, just a year before he passed away. He had such a beautiful smile. Look at him for me, will you, love? Tell me, is he still smiling?'

Moira looked at the gilt frame on the wall and the space where the image of Doris's late husband had faded to white in the sunlight.

'Yes,' answered, Moira, 'he's still smiling.'

# Almost Persuaded

From deep behind the heavy door Patsy Cline was singing The Honky Tonk Merry Go Round accompanied by slide guitar and tinkling ivories. A brief hesitation, then warmth and light flooded momentarily into the street as the square-shouldered figure pushed open the door and entered.

From inside, the voice wasn't quite Patsy Cline. Good, though, Hicks thought, as he heaved his weight onto a bar stool, nodding in the direction of the 'Bud on tap' sign and flipping a ten from his hip pocket onto the bar. After six days on the road his eyelids were heavy; it was as if he didn't see the hand that wiped the mahogany veneer with a cloth, placed a glass on a paper napkin and exchanged the ten for a five, a one, a quarter. As he took a gulp through the froth, he caught Doc Watson smiling at him from a faded signed photo behind the bar, a phony smile collecting dust in a tarnished frame. Above it a mirror revealed the singer, coal black hair cascading from a cowgirl hat, sequined jacket casting sparkles in his direction. She was into the next song and her eyes seemed to pick up his reflection as she sang, 'Turn the cards slowly while you're dealing, darling.' Swivelling on the stool, he cast his most fetching smile in her direction, neatly emulating the framed portrait. The way she moved brought back a box of memories: the hint of a ruby smile, the curve of a breast, slender fingers curling round a microphone. Now she was definitely looking in his direction. 'So where do I go from here?' he wondered, pushing his empty glass across the bar. 'Just don't let her know she's getting through to you, that's all. Life is just heartaches by the numbers, but who's counting?'

The song over, she stepped down, 'thank ye all'-ing the less than appreciative audience, heading straight for the bar. An aspiring George Jones replaced her at the microphone and launched into a waltz: 'Last night all alone in a ballroom ...'

She seemed to float across the floor, taking up a position on the stool next to Hicks. 'Nice,' she said, indicating the 'HH' on the breast pocket of his braided shirt. 'Hickory Holler original,' he replied, not taking his eyes off her. The vocals flowed over from the stage, '...and as she pressed her soft hand in mine, I found myself wanting to kiss her, for temptation was flowing like wine...' More drinks appeared on the bar, the dwindling pile of bills being replaced by small change. The growing hubbub drowned their conversation, the no-longer new crystal chandeliers barely lighting up the paintings on the wall, the soft light adding an intimacy to the smoke-filled atmosphere of the bar room. Polite conversation turned into laughter, trembling lips formed into a genuine smile; a soft hand touched his, and as they left the bar for the cool darkness of the night, he placed an arm round her shoulders.

'The funny thing is,' he sighed, as the saloon door closed behind them, 'this time I didn't even get to Albuquerque.'

'It makes no difference now,' she smiled, hooking her arm in his, 'Let's go home.'

— ❧ ❧ —

# The Rocking Horse

'There's something in the attic.'

'Don't be silly. There can't be anything up there.'

'Yes, there is. Come and look.'

That was easier said than done. In the little old terraced house they had just moved into as part of their downsizing project, the loft access was nothing more than an inspection hatch, just large enough for one person to put their head through and shine a torch into the cobwebbed recesses. There was no skylight, only the disorienting dance of darting shadows, a shadowplay in which objects seem to flit in and out of existence.

Cautiously, Adrian climbed down the wobbly aluminium stepladder and handed her the torch. Reluctantly, Debbie ascended, making sure that Adrian was keeping the ladder steady. With her head in the darkness, she flashed the torch, glanced from side to side, and descended almost immediately.

'There's nothing there. You couldn't get anything up there. The hatch is too small.'

'Yes, there is. There's a trunk.'

'Yeah, yeah – there's always a trunk in an attic.'

'And a rocking horse.'

At least, this elicited an incredulous laugh.

'Well, I'll believe you on the trunk, because my eyes aren't so good, but a rocking horse? Come off it. No way.'

'I'll prove it.'

'Oh, yeah, and how?'

'We'll have the hatch made bigger, get a loft ladder fitted and take a proper look.'

'Suit yourself.'

And that's what they did. A phone call to a local loft conversion company, one visit to measure up and then another one to replace the hatch with a proper trapdoor and fit a folding staircase, and it was all done.

Debbie showed little interest after once again exploring by torchlight. She refused to take the last few steps and clamber through onto the grimy old floorboards. Still, she saw nothing but shadows. And in any case, the tight confines of the attic and low beams meant that only one person could venture through the trapdoor at any one time.

Adrian, however, no longer had any interest in convincing her. He knew what he could see, and he had the feeling that it was calling to him. Only him.

As he ascended the ladder and passed through the hatch, he found that he no longer needed the torch he still clutched in his hand. Where the light was coming from, he could not tell; it permeated the attic without emanating from any particular place, a steady glow that became brighter as he took the final step and stood on the old dusty floorboards. And now he could see them both clearly, a painted rocking horse and an ancient leather-clad trunk.

As he stepped closer to the rocking horse, he could feel its essence, the spirit of childhood beckoning to him.

'Come closer,' said the horse, 'let me take you back.'

He reached out, touched its painted mane and his heart leapt as he was filled with the presence of happy, joyful days, days of untroubled mirth and laughter, long past but living on in the heart – oh, to have those days back. Days of innocence and bliss, of sweets and chocolate, of magical games and fantastic adventures on horseback, of riding over the prairie, thundering over the terrain with the mavericks, thrashing through the thickets in hot pursuit of friend or foe on a fantastic quest sure to end in fame wealth and the admiration of all. Oh, to relive those times! Would it not be wonderful?

Shaken by what he had seen, by the images that had briefly taken hold of him, he drew his hand away and felt his gaze drawn to the trunk. Should he open it? Look inside? His fingers traced a path through the dust on its lid, reaching for the latch that kept its contents a mystery, but a tingling sensation passed through his fingers, his hand, his arm, becoming ever fiercer, causing him to gasp and his heart to beat faster, faster as the power of the trunk took hold, then slower, slower, ever slower, as the spirit of old age washed over him and the trunk containing a lifetime of forgotten memories revealed its secrets – faded photographs of people no living soul can identify, bric-à-brac and keepsakes that have lost their lustre and their meaning, blending with the dust that has fallen on them, their origins lost in the mist of receding memory.

He withdrew his hand from the lid of the trunk and once again the rocking horse called to him, promising laughter and happy, carefree days, but the trunk, too, reached out, enticing, soothing, begging him to choose a life fulfilled, lasting contentment. Kneeling now between the trunk and the rocking horse, he covered his face with both hands, trying to retain his strength in the struggle between two elemental forces.

Now for the first and only time in his life, he was being offered a choice between the chaotic joy of everlasting childhood and the soothing, fulfilling calm of eternal oblivion. Slowly, he uncovered his face, looked from one manifestation to the other, and reached out his hand.

Debbie was busy cleaning and tidying up, as one does when getting ready to move out, when she noticed that the trapdoor to the loft was open, access provided by a folding staircase. Strange. There never used to be a staircase there. Or if there was, it had never been used. Perhaps one of the workmen had left the trapdoor open. Yes, that would be it. Such untidy people. The spring-loaded stairs folded easily as she took hold of the lower part and raised it toward the hatch. It fitted so snugly in place, you would never even notice it was there. The only clue was a small pile of dust on the carpet.

With a sigh, she took the vacuum cleaner out of the closet and set about removing all traces of the access to the space above. After living alone all these years, it was just another of those little chores. Sometimes she imagined that she had married, that she had shared this house with a loving husband, but it was never to be; just one of those things. Anyway, the house itself was company enough.

# The Seasonal Visitor

The fire in the hearth was burning low as the silent whisper of a chill wind hissed through the cracks in the windowpanes. The snow on the gloomy hills muffled all sounds from outside; only the ticking of the clock on the mantelpiece disturbed the silence. A glance told Gwyneth that it was one minute to twelve – sixty seconds to the end of what had not been a good year.

Images flashed through her mind – the accident, the hospital, the solemn procession through the churchyard and the final farewell. At first, people had been understanding, supportive, consoling her for her loss, but slowly the harsh realities of life had begun to pile up. The promise to keep her job open had come to nothing when the advertising agency had been taken over. She had even been turned away by the new supermarket looking for part-time staff. The initial flow of understanding letters from relatives and friends had faded away, leaving only a mounting pile of bills and final demands. The unopened newspaper lay on the floor where she had discarded it yesterday. What was the point in even looking at the situations vacant anymore? No-one wanted a burned-out graphic designer.

The minute hand on the clock joined the hour hand at the top of the dial. The fire flickered a little and seemed to go dark for a moment as the icy wind increased its pitch to a high whine before fading away completely. Then the room seemed to become warmer, lighter, as though caught in the glow of a giant candle.

At first, she did not see him standing by the mantelpiece, and when she did she was too overcome by surprise to utter a word. A deep intake of breath as joy mixed with fear left her speechless, mouth gaping. It was as if she could both see Daniel and see through him at the same time, but then this vapid quality seemed to vanish as he moved towards her.

When she found her voice, it was little more than a whimper, 'Is it really you?'

Daniel smiled, took her hands, gently pulling her to her feet.

'Hello, honey,' he said, 'I'm here to give you your strength back.'

It was the old familiar lilt, the sparkle in the eyes that she thought she had lost forever.

'Oh, Daniel,' she sobbed as she fell into his arms.

'Hush,' he said gently stroking her cheek, 'Let's not waste time. They only let me do this once a year.'

Together they drifted towards the staircase …

When she awoke the next morning, it was as if all the songbirds of spring were outside her window. Pulling the curtains apart, she looked out over the winter landscape and tore open the window. A sudden breeze caused something on the floor to flutter at the corner of her eye – the newspaper. It was open at the jobs page and one of the announcements was ringed in red ink. 'Graphic Designer needed urgently. Excellent pay and prospects.' In the margin was a handwritten note 'Try this. Tell me all about it next year.' The handwriting was Daniel's.

— ❧ ❧ —

# A Knight's Tale

## Scene One

'What time are we on?'

'Ten minutes to go, Sir Cieran.'

'Are you sure I don't need makeup? I must look a mess.'

'No, you're fine. Just think of it as a casual chat with friends. Pretty much like Skyping your grandchildren.'

'As bad as that? Last time, nine-year old Juliet asked me if I had ever met The Grand Wizard of Strom and when I said, but honey, I AM the Grand Wizard of Strom, she just said, yeah, yeah and pulled a face.'

'Well, you can't expect her to understand that her Gramps is an Oscar-winning actor who doesn't look a bit like some of the characters he plays. Anyway, this evening will be a doddle,' reassured the unflappable Steph, the star's long-time dresser, personal assistant and willing factotum, deftly running a soft brush across the actor's thinning hair. 'All you have to do is chat informally with Julian about your career, your days at the Royal Shakespeare Company and the forthcoming live tour. And it's much nicer to do it here from your own home rather than head downtown to the studio.'

'It would have been nice to do this in a theatre, though. You don't get the interaction with video conferencing.'

'Ah, but you don't have far to go after the show either. And Robin and Marion will be online, too, so you can swap stories about your charity work.'

'And what about the audience. Did you say they get to ask questions, too?'

'Yes, but only in chat mode. They can see you, but you can't see them. And you don't have to answer anything that you don't want to. Julian will vet the questions first and run them past you.'

Sir Cieran pursed his lips and raised his eyebrows, a clown-like facial gesture that formed part of his usual warm-up routine in the dressing room. It made him look even more helpless than he felt. The stage was fine, supported by a whole team of backstage workers, TV and movie were second nature to him. He could easily perform in front of a team of camera operators, sound technicians and the dozens of other people involved in making movies, but somehow, this was more daunting. A tiny webcam mounted on a computer monitor was all that he had to play to.

'Do you know, after all these years, I still get butterflies before I go on. Do you think I could have a stiff gin?'

'Later, dear, later,' soothed Steph, 'We're on in a moment.' The familiar figure of Julian Yates appeared in a rectangle on the screen, Sir's own live mirror image in another rectangle beside him. Then they were joined by one of the other celebrity guests for this evening's show, the dapper Robin Thwaite, Sir's occasional co-star on stage and screen.

'Ready for this?' asked Robin.

'We'll see, won't we?' replied Sir, shifting his position to improve the framing. And at that moment, the familiar face of Marion Reed popped into existence, too, her ever-gracious smile melting his heart as it had done all those years ago.

'Hello, ducky,' she mouthed, still on mute, sharing one of their old jokes.

Steph was speaking to an invisible technical host on another device, counting down:

'Five minutes... positions everybody... all set... ready to roll... okay, Ken, you can let the audience in now.'

## Scene Two

Five minutes to go. It would be an exaggeration to say that Raglan had waited all his life for this moment, but it was a pretty big one all the same. Sir Cieran Kelley, also known as Sir C or to his friends, the joke ran, simply as Sir, was due to appear in a live streaming broadcast billed as 'A Knight's Tale.' A role model to many in the entertainment industry, the singing, dancing star of 'From Nowhere to Eternity' and grizzled wizard from the 'Highest Tower' series of fantasy movies had launched his stage career as the youngest ever Hamlet to tour with the Royal Shakespeare Company. And Raglan had been there. At the age of sixteen, it was his first ever visit to the theatre – and it turned out to be a life-changing event. Not in the sense that he had ever become an actor himself or gone into show business in any form, but it was simply a magical experience that had lodged itself firmly in his psyche. He could remember every glorious minute of that performance and had followed Cieran Kelley's career ever since, rejoiced in his double Oscar and subsequent knighthood, vicariously proud of his idol's tireless work on behalf of developing countries and opening up the world of the arts and the theatre in particular to a new generation of theatre-goers, many of whom were shocked at first and then won over by the sight of actors in the flesh rather than the digital images they had grown up with.

And now, in a sense, Sir Cieran was going to become a digital image himself, but he would still be there live – in person. Not theatre, that's true, but not impersonal television either. He would be there in person, ready to answer questions from the audience, maybe even, from Raglan.

## Scene Three

'So, Robin, what do you remember about meeting Sir Cieran for the first time?'

'Ah, well, that would be over 50 years ago. I was working front of house at the Aldwych Theatre and Cieran here was appearing in...'

The compere had neatly turned Robin Thwaite, a megastar in his own right, onto a favourite anecdote which he had surely told a thousand times before but managed to make fresh and exciting each time, like an intimate revelation of his first encounter with a future star which would eventually burgeon into a lifetime friendship.

Indeed, Raglan had heard the story so many times that he relished in the slight variations that entered into the narrative each time it was told. Sometimes it was the Aldwych, sometimes the Haymarket, sometimes front of house and sometimes the box office, but the essence of the story was always the same, always it was a fleeting encounter that left a lasting impression on the young Robin, awakening the desire in him to rise to such heights himself one day.

Anecdotes and stories, reminiscences and an occasional appeal on behalf the charitable organisations filled the next hour so before Julian opened up the forum and invited questions:

'And now we open up the discussion to our online audience. Please type your questions into chat and we will convey them to Sir Cieran, who will answer as many as he possibly can in the time we have left.

Hesitatingly, Raglan's fingers hovered over the keyboard, then he typed: 'Do you have any recollections of your performance in Hamlet at the Abbey Theatre sixty years ago this week? And please accept the belated apologies from a small boy who had a coughing fit in the middle of the famous monologue and almost interrupted the performance?'

Several questions were read out and answered, in some cases earnestly and in others eliciting a humorous but good-natured comment and occasion for banter between the on-screen celebrities.

'Here's an interesting one,' said Julian with a smile, 'from an audience member in County

Antrim – and he read out Raglan's question.'

Raglan stared transfixed at the screen as Sir Cieran smiled thoughtfully, wistfully, eyes looking ever so slightly upwards into the lids in a subtle gesture of recall.

'Do you know,' mused Sir, 'I do remember that. And I'm pleased to say it didn't put me off my stride. And I would like to say hello to that small boy if he is here tonight. I have often wondered what happened to the mysterious coughing boy. It's precisely what we need today, more young people in the theatre. Thank you for being there all those years ago.'

Raglan was stunned. Not only did Sir remember that night but had even thanked him for being there. The rest of the show took its course and Raglan duly applauded at the end, but he wasn't really aware of the closing remarks. His elbows on the desk in front of the monitor, palms supporting his chin, he stared at the closing message on the screen. It was hard to describe what he felt. It was a sense of mission accomplished, an ambition achieved. He uttered an extended sigh of, not exactly relief, maybe of fulfilment, maybe of joy. It was difficult to say. The only thing that could be said with certainty, is that it was precisely at this point that his heart stopped, his head still resting in his palms, his unseeing eyes still directed at the screen.

## Scene Four

Steph clicked the 'End Session' button and turned to Sir Cieran, deftly removing the throat mike and almost simultaneously pouring him a stiff gin and tonic.

'Do you really remember that small boy and his coughing fit?' she asked.

Sir Cieran smiled his engaging smile and looked directly at his friend and confidante and with a gentle sigh, replied:

'Does it really matter?'

# Digital Flashback

To conclude this collection of strange tales, I have added three previously unpublished stories featuring the use of computers in the home but written at a time when digital technologies were in their infancy. They are presented here in reverse order of writing, each story stepping a bit further back in time.

**Game On** is set at the turn of the millennium, before the advent of multi-player online gaming, **The Betamorphosis** is a Kafka pastiche set in the early nineties and the final story, **Two's Company**, was written sometime around 1982 when the Commodore VIC-20 home computer had just been launched. This compact piece of kit was aimed firmly at the domestic market and was the first device of its kind to sell a million units.

At a time when computers were generally found only in large corporations and universities, the idea of having a computer of any kind in the home was quite revolutionary, and the concept of the internet was many years away.

# Game On

## LEVEL ONE

Des stared at the monitor.

LOVE  OR  MONEY?

The cursor wavered over the two options. He moved it towards the MONEY icon.

From the kitchen came the sound of pots and pans, the smell of baking, the gush of a water tap.

On the screen a dollar bill and a heart flashed alternately.

CHOOSE  NOW
OR  I  WILL  CHOOSE  FOR
YOU.

Des liked games with clear results, scores in points, dollars, pounds, euros. On the other hand, he was getting a bit bored by games like Casino3000, Money-poly and the like.

'Mash or fries?' called his wife Sonja from the adjacent kitchen.

'Roast spuds,' he replied without thinking and at that moment his finger made an almost imperceptible movement and clicked on the mouse button.

The heart enlarged to fill the screen.

```
YOU HAVE THREE LIVES.
   CLICK TO START.
```

Click.

```
ENTER YOUR NAME.
```

"Des"

```
AGE?
```

"28"

```
SINGLE OR MARRIED?
```

He clicked on MARRIED.

```
YOU HAVE CHOSEN LOVE.
THIS IS AN ADVENTURE
       GAME.
YOU HAVE TWO LIVES
       LEFT.
```

Damn!

SINGLE OR MARRIED?

In other words, do you want to play, or not? He hesitated.

Click.

He stared at the screen. Nothing happened. Tried to move the cursor. Nothing happened. That was odd. This machine had never hung up before. He clicked on the 'webcam' button on the task bar.

The screen showed him at the computer, the image mimicking his movements. He clicked again. Nothing happened. Maybe the game has one of those patience functions, he thought. Leave it for a few minutes and see if anything happens. A cup of tea would be nice, though.

'Sonja!'

Then he noticed that it was oddly quiet. He stood up, shook his head as you sometimes do to clear it when the world is getting to much and went into the kitchen. Stopped dead, jaw hanging. The kitchen was reasonably tidy but seemed somehow different, disorganised, Sonja can't be far away. The smell of baking was still there. A half-opened packet of instant mash stood on the worktop. He had asked for roasts. The best thing to go with Sonja's home-baked steak pies. Somehow the smell wasn't right, sort of scorched. In a flash of realisation, he opened the oven, grabbed an oven glove and whipped out the supermarket-bought meat pie still in its clear plastic foil wrapping which was now turning an ugly brown as the smell of baking plastic filled the kitchen.

Damn! He flung it in the bin as usual.

As usual? But Sonja...?

It was as if his legs gave way. He didn't so much sit down at the kitchen table as land on the chair with a thud. The only chair. He looked around the kitchen again. Things were missing. Spices. Recipe books. Bottles of things. Little fluffy things. The list above the fridge. Sonja must have taken it with her when she went shopping. Other things were wrong, too. She had left her laptop on the kitchen table. She never did that, especially not when she was cooking. He looked over to the corner where she always put her shopping basket when she came in. In place of the wicker basket were two carrier bags from the supermarket. He stared at them for a moment, trying to fill in the blanks in his head, then went over and took out the contents, spread them on the table, a cool chill running through his body as he stared at the seemingly random collection of packaged foods – ready meals for one, just microwave for three minutes; cans of beans, goulash, mixed veg; pot noodles; a wilting frozen pizza in a plastic foil wrapping; a six pack of beer.

He sat. Thought. Stood up. Went back to the study and looked at the monitor. The dumb, stupid, silent, arrogant flat screen monitor staring at him. But all he saw was his own face staring back at him as he stared at the web cam.

Right.

Back in the kitchen he switched on Sonja's laptop. No, *his* laptop. He had bought it because of the presentation he needed to give at the company's next in-house training seminar. Even though he worked for a major software manufacturer, he still had to buy his own equipment. The laptop was linked to his desktop machine by a Wireless LAN. The screen showed him switching on the laptop. But that was impossible. There was no web cam here. On the other hand, nothing was impossible. Life was a game. He had said so often enough himself. He stared at the screen.

What do I have to do?

He thought hard. There was only one obvious answer: Get her back.

He recalled how they had met at the company's annual dinner dance. That had been five years ago. Whether it was love at first sight or not, he couldn't say, but it had certainly been a whirlwind romance. And now they were happily married – except that they weren't. The more he thought about it, the more it became clear to him. He hadn't gone to the dance; he had stayed at home, installing a new games interface. After all it was an important project for the computer firm he worked for. And he hated the company's events. They seated you at a table with complete strangers and expected you to get on with them. Des didn't get on well with people he didn't know. Maybe because he didn't know many people.

Des spent the rest of the day moping around the flat (Flat? Didn't we have a house?) and preparing himself inwardly for his presentation tomorrow. That girl would be there. From the northern office.

She was one of the presenters at the previous seminar, but he had never had the chance to talk to her. What was her name again? Sandra? Sandy? Sonja? That was it. Something tugged at the back of his mind. Maybe he should ask her out sometime. Ask her out? Didn't that sound rather old-fashioned? He wouldn't even know how to go about it. And as for 'sometime' - she would be at the seminar tomorrow, but after that he would probably never see her again. Ever. No, wait a minute, wasn't there something else? He stared at the five empty cans of lager and popped the sixth, reached for the TV remote control and before he knew it, he was fast asleep.

## LEVEL TWO

'So, what did you think.'

'Of your presentation. Great. Loved the bit about the new interface. Don't really see how it can be done, but you certainly made me want to know more.'

'That's great,' said Des, catching his breath just slightly as she smiled. Everything about her seemed somehow familiar.

'Er... listen. This is a bit awkward; I mean I know we've only just met, but...'

As far as she could tell, her smile was genuine, but Sonja also had a puzzled look as she gently put down her white, corporate-issue coffee cup on the bistro-style table they stood at.

He hadn't realised he was sweating, but now he felt the beads chill as they trickled down his face. In another five minutes, the coffee-break would be over, and he may never get another chance.

'...but what?' Clearly, she needed him to say it.

'Well, I was wondering if you would like to go out to dinner sometime?'

It sounded lame, but it was the best he could do. And at least she didn't laugh. Or slap him in the face. Not quite.

'Well, that's very nice of you,' she smiled, 'but you do realise, don't you, that I'm married? I think I'll pass.'

The room swam. The world turned around him. The giddiness forced him to close his eyes. He was back in the kitchen, staring at the screen of the laptop.

It showed him staring open-mouthed at Sonja as she fingered her coffee-cup. The image faded and showed him back in the kitchen.

ONE LIFE LEFT.

Damn!

Of course, he couldn't win her back by approaching her as she is now. Her life had moved on. They had never met. If they had met five years ago, she would be here now, but clearly, she had met someone else instead.

He needed to think. Above all, he needed another six-pack.

The supermarket was just on the corner, one of those with just half a dozen checkouts, big enough to stock anything a single guy wants and small enough to be in and out quickly without having to hunt through miles of shelves for a few simple supplies. And Des had his regular checkout girl there, too. Not that they had ever exchanged more than a word or too, although he knew that her name was Carol. After all, it was on a badge pinned to her breast.

When he had been married to Sonja (Sonja? Who was Sonja? Must be fantasising again), he had never really noticed the girl at the checkout, but now he realised that he always chose her queue, even when the others were shorter. As he did now. Somehow his imagination seemed to be playing tricks on him. She seemed to recognise him as he reached the front of the queue. Her eyelids fluttered just a little, her fingers seemed nervous as she passed his purchases over the barcode reader. Six pack. Beep. A two-litre bottle of Coke. Beep. Chicken dinner ready meal. Nothing. Again. Nothing. She flashed him a smile.

'Sorry. Just a minute.' She inclined her head, lips close to a microphone on a stalk. 'Price needed at till six.' She looked up. 'Sorry,' she said again.

'That's OK.'

Des shifted nervously, felt he ought to say more and then realised something. She knew a lot more about him than he did about her. Knew that he was single for one thing – all those ready meals – a non-smoker – never touched the cigarettes on offer at the till – drank lager – and God knows what else she knew. But then, again, why should she be interested? Again, she bent over the microphone:

'Price please, till six.' And then to the queue behind Des: 'Could you go to the next checkout, please.'

Des shifted again uneasily. 'I could leave that here, if you don't have a price for it,' he said.

'It'll just take a minute,' she said in a business-like, neutral tone, then, as if regretting something, 'I wouldn't want you to miss your dinner.' And a smile. A real smile.

'Well, I don't really like eating alone, anyway,' he said.

### LEVEL THREE

Whenever Carol came home from the super-market, it was as though a dozen Christmases had arrived at once. She spent the first ten minutes unpacking bargains, special offers and things bought on the staff discount scheme and chattering about value for money and unbeatable prices. She was so bubbly, it was infectious, so different from the shy, serious Carol who worked at the checkout. Des just wanted to take her in his arms and lead her straight to the bedroom. In fact, he often did. She would continue to bubble away for a while with all that energy, the same energy that she channelled into their relationship, but would slowly transcend into yet another Carol, the one who combined gentle caressing tenderness with mad, passionate lovemaking.

Today was one of those days. It was still early evening, but they were already in bed, satisfied, snuggling. Tomorrow was a holiday, so they could lie in as long as they wanted. Carol raised her head, gave him that special smile.

'I'm so happy.'

'Me too.'

'I love you so much.'

'I love you, too.'

'Really. Do you really, really, really?' in her childish giggling way.

'I really, really do.'

'And you've never loved anybody else like you love me?'

'Never. You're the only one.' He leaned over to kiss her, but she wasn't there.

He was staring at his own face in the monitor.

On top of the image the words were flashing.

```
        GAME  OVER.
PLAY  AGAIN?  (YES/NO)
```

That was all.

Damn!

He stared at the screen, paralysed.

```
        GAME  OVER.
```

So, had he won or lost?

Something wafted through the air, reached his nostrils. A voice came from the kitchen:

'OK. Roast spuds it is.'

He sat there for a long time.

```
    PLAY  AGAIN?
    (YES  /  NO)
```

He reached over and clicked on NO.

The image vanished and was replaced by the regular system interface.

Next time he would go for the money. Definitely.

# The Betamorphosis

One morning Francis woke up and found himself transformed into a monstrous operating system. 'What's wrong with me?' he squeaked in a mouse-like voice. Everything in his bedroom seemed normal, albeit a little out of focus; it was as though the world were made up of tiny dots that wouldn't quite keep still, and there were a number of strange symbols running across his line of sight: a folder, a printer, disks, scissors, even a pair of binoculars. What they were doing there, he had no idea. He certainly could not look through them. It was disconcerting, to say the least, so he closed his eyes.

Everything went blank, except for a capital 'c' and a funny kind of bracket at the top left of his field of vision. In panic, Francis opened his eyes again. Now everywhere he looked there was a funny kind of pointer, like a misplaced arrowhead aiming nowhere in particular. He tried to sit up in bed but found he could not move. He strained to raise his arm, but nothing happened except that the pointer followed his glance. This gave him an idea. He focused hard on his hand, so that the arrow was pointing at the tip of his finger and slowly panned his gaze along his arm. As he did so, his arm seemed to turn black, and he found that in this condition he could move his body, one piece at a time, to a new position. Limb by limb, he struggled out of bed and reached for his spectacles. In order to put them on his nose he first had to mark them as he had done with his body and then with a click they slotted into place. He gave a boyish smile as the world came into better focus, pleased at this demonstration of his genius. But his joy was short-lived, for now the pointer refused to move, and his eyes became locked in a glassy stare. A message flashed in front of his spectacles: 'Beta version only. Peripherals not supported.'

Unable to move, the genius stood there with a puerile grin frozen on his face, waiting for them to take him away.

# Two's Company

## 1. Give them an inch...

It began during the holidays. Salena and Trapps Mackenzie had decided to spend the two weeks at home to sort out a few things around the house, and generally to spare themselves the exertion of dashing off on an official holiday. For Salena it meant little change anyway, as she did not go out to work, but she had sworn to take things a little easier and to spend more time with her studies, an external degree program in the social sciences. By the end of the year, perhaps, she would have completed the final units and be well on her way to a new career. Trapps too had his hobby. He had always been fascinated by robots and computers and artificial intelligence, and had taken the opportunity at a recent trade fair of buying a new model home computer. For the next couple of weeks, he would have time to get acquainted with his new acquisition.

At first Salena took little notice of the unprepossessing little machine sitting in the corner of the lounge. She accepted that it was Trapps' hobby and would keep him happy for a while, besides giving her the chance to do some much-needed reading. He could sit in front of the thing as long as he wanted, leaving her free to read, do the housework, and relax a little in the evenings in front of a quiet fire.

The trouble started when she found herself sitting alone, staring at her husband's empty place because he could not tear himself away from that pretty screen and whatever was on it.

Even after she had spent hours one day preparing his favourite casserole. had she found it impossible to entice him away from his flickering new toy.

'What on earth has gotten into you? You've hardly slept or eaten anything for days, and I've just wasted the whole afternoon in the kitchen cooking for two when I should have been cooking for one.'

'Or three,' murmured Trapps, hardly turning his face from the screen. 'Victor is almost human, you know.'

'Victor!' she screamed, 'you've even given the blasted thing a name now, have you? Well, you can damn well marry your computer. I'm going out.'

Unperturbed, Trapps tapped away at the keyboard as the door slammed behind his wife. On the screen there appeared the legend,

```
NEVER MIND, TRAPPS. EN-
   TER THE NEXT FUNCTION
   AND WE'LL CONTINUE OUR
            PROGRAM.
```

Happily, Trapps keyed in a code and waited patiently for the response. He didn't even notice the darkness slowly seeping into the room from outside until only Victor and himself were visible in a small corner of the large lounge, bathed in the friendly glow of Victor's Visual Display Unit.

As dawn was breaking, and a world somewhere out there was stirring dreamily from sleep, Trapps barely acknowledged the front door latch slide open and Salena's footsteps trippling gently upstairs. Only her scream from the bedroom interrupted his concentration. When he reached the top of the stairs, she was in tears.

'Oh, that's just fine!' she sobbed, 'Here am I worried sick that you'll be angry or upset because I've been out all night, and where are you? Down there playing with your Goddamn adding machine! You probably didn't even notice I'd gone.'

'Course I did, darling,' he soothed, 'I've been worried about you. Where have you been?' He tried to inject a mixture of concern and anger into his voice, but was conscious that it did not quite come off.

'Fucking the whole regiment of Guards,' she retorted, storming past him into the bathroom. Trapps glanced into the bedroom at a borrowed coat that lay on the floor. Then he said,

'Ah, you've been to your sister's, I suppose.' He ignored the clattering of a plastic tumbler against the bathroom door and padded quietly back downstairs.

## 2. If you can't beat 'em...

Salena's sister Jackie had always been the pragmatic one. 'Look,' she said, 'if that machine is driving a wedge between you and Trapps, then why don't you get him to show you what it does? At least that way, he'll have to talk to you.'

Reluctantly, Salena agreed to give it a try. At first Trapps was rather brutish, domineering but condescending, explaining odd aspects of programming in a tone that pretty much said, 'Now, you won't understand this anyway, but since you ask, I'll blind you with science.' Only he very soon found that he couldn't blind her with science. For the first time, he realised that she was far from dumb. After all, she was on her way to a degree in, what was it? Social Sciences? She was quite an adaptable girl. He explained a few things. She understood. Reluctantly, he explained more. She sat down at the keyboard, touched the little plastic keys and Victor sprang to life. She looked at the screen. The phrase,


```
HI!  GOOD  TO  SEE  YOU
         AGAIN.
```

appeared on it. She looked and she saw. Her nimble fingers called up the listing and changed a. few lines of program. The word 'again' disappeared from the display, and a few seconds later, Victor added,

```
    IT'S NICE TO HAVE
    SOMEONE NEW AROUND
         HERE.
```

She looked, and she understood. Trapps hovered behind her, making encouraging noises and talking about advanced programming techniques. She wasn't listening. She didn't need to. Victor was already teaching her everything she wanted to know.

Soon Trapps' holiday was over and he had to return to work, leaving Victor cold and unattended, silent and morose in the corner of the lounge, whilst the gentle rise and fall of Salena's breast under the covers suggested she was sleeping. But no sooner had the latch of the garden gate clicked home, than the bed was empty and Victor's rectangular face aglow with new life.

There were no arguments for a long time after Trapps' return to work. When he came home in the evening, Salena was humming busily in the kitchen and did not even object if he sat right down in front of the computer. She even brought him food on a tray and smiled understandingly. Only sometimes did he wonder why the section of the plastic casing that housed the transformer was somewhat warmer than he might have expected.

## 3. What's good for the goose...

Harmony prevailed. The couple related quite happily through and around the computer. Sometimes Trapps would leave little messages for her on the screen, and occasionally she would buy odd accessories for him to use with the machine. He was obviously delighted at the pleasure she had in seeing him rig up new gadgets to Victor's central processing unit, such as the modem which enabled access to Victor's main logic system via a normal telephone line. Victor could even be programmed to make or receive telephone calls – to or from another computer, of course.

'What are you working on now?' asked Salena one Sunday as Trapps sat poised over the dismantled keyboard, leads, plugs and cables about his feet.

'I'm connecting an audio link to the telephone modem.'

'What's that good for?'

'It will enable the computer to give audio responses over the telephone.'

'You mean it will be able to talk?'

'Not exactly, but you'll be able to hear the sort of bleeps and blips you get with an arcade game, and if you know the code, then you can virtually understand them like speech.'

She gave him his coffee and smiled, 'That's nice.'

Several times during the following week, Trapps tried to make contact with Victor through the telephone link but could raise nothing better than an engaged tone. Perhaps there was a malfunction of some kind, or a fault in the program. If so, he would have to get it checked. But first he must ask Salena.

'Say, were you on the phone today? I couldn't get through.'

'No, why? What did you ring about?'

'Oh, I didn't want to speak to you. I tried to get through to Victor.'

If he had looked at her eyes at that moment, the course of their lives might have been altered, but already he was staring at the screen again, and barely heard her say,

'Oh, yes, that's right. Jackie phoned. We talked for a long time. I forgot.'

Trapps touched the console. It was hot.

'You've been using my computer!' he exploded, 'So that's it! That's why you've been so sweet to me all this time. You've been messing around with Victor!'

'For God's sake, Trapps, it's only a machine!'

'Don't you dare say that, you cheating little bitch! Get the Hell out of here!'

For the first time in their married life, he struck her, violently, across the face.

'Well, stuff you,' she screamed back, 'I've just about had enough of you. You spend all your free time sitting there yourself. I'm through. One of you has to go.'

'What do you mean, "one of us"?' he bellowed, but once again the door had slammed. This time she did not come back. And this time he did worry.

'The bitch!' thought Trapps as he sat down at the console. 'If I could find her personal code, I could work out what she has been doing with Victor.' His expert fingers soon had the initial code, and Victor responded:

```
HELLO, DARLING!
```

Furiously, jealously, Trapp's fingers pumped the keys. His heart pounded as he tried to access Victor's responses and reactions. What on earth had she been playing at?

## 4. All good things...

'Have you left him for good, then?' asked Jackie, after hearing Salena's tale.

'It's not a matter of that,' replied her sister, 'but I'm afraid he may have some kind of accident. That machine can be dangerous, you know.'

'Oh, come on! Still, I'm amazed that you're so calm after such a scene with him, Fancy slapping you about like that. Your face is all red and your eye is blackening.'

'It doesn't matter,' said Salena. 'It doesn't hurt now. Do you mind if I use your phone?'

'Go right ahead, but I don't know why you want to call him.'

Salena dialled and listened for a moment to the apparently incoherent bleeps from the receiver, aimlessly tapping her fingernails on the mouthpiece. Then she hung up.

'No answer,' she said, 'he isn't home.'

'Or he's busy playing with his machine,' said Jackie scornfully.

'Possibly, possibly,' mused Salena and sat down, calm at last.

One of the peripherals of the VCT personal computer is a high frequency generator capable of producing sounds well beyond the range of human hearing. Such tones may be used to trigger off supplementary electrical apparatus after the manner of a TV remote control unit, but such a device must be used with caution, for an error in programming, or a few extra instructions, and the range can be extended to an ear-splitting frequency that shatters the eardrums and penetrates the brain, with potentially fatal consequences.

On the other end of the telephone line, Victor gave a few excited bleeps as the frequencies he had been emitting returned to within the range of human hearing. On the floor in front of him lay the crumpled body of one Trapps Mackenzie, a trickle of blood oozing from each ear, whilst on the screen, flashing intermittently, appeared just one word:

TERMINATED